I Wanna Iguana

KAREN KAUFMAN ORLOFF • ILLUSTRATED BY DAVID CATROW

SCHOLASTIC INC.

New York Toronto London Auckland Sydney
Mexico City New Delhi Hong Kong Buenos Aires

ISBN 0-439-80015-3

Text copyright © 2004 by Karen Kaufman Orloff.
Illustrations copyright © 2004 by David Catrow. All rights reserved.
Published by Scholastic Inc., 557 Broadway, New York, NY 10012, by arrangement with G. P. Putnam's Sons, an imprint of Penguin Putnam Books for Young Readers, a division of Penguin Group (USA) Inc. SCHOLASTIC and associated logos are trademarks and/or registered trademarks of Scholastic Inc.

12 11 10 9 8 7 6 5 4 3 2   5 6 7 8 9 10/0

Printed in the U.S.A.   40

First Scholastic printing, September 2005

Designed by Marikka Tamura. Text set in Catchup and Comic Sans.
The art was done in pencil and watercolor.

To Max and Emily
for their inspiration,
to Brad for his support,
and to all my writer friends
for making me work harder. —K.K.O.

To Mr. Alexander—
you taught me discipline
and how to be an artist. —D.C.

Dear Mom,

I know you don't think I should have Mikey Gulligan's baby iguana have Mikey Gulligan's baby iguana, but here's why I should. I think I should when he moves, he goes to Stinky and when he moves, he goes to Stinky and If I don't take it, will eat it. If I don't take it, he goes to Stinky and Stinky's dog, Lurch, will eat it. You don't want that to happen, do you?

Signed,
Your sensitive son,
Alex

Dear Alex,

I'm glad you're so compassionate,
but I doubt that Stinky's mother
will let Lurch get into
the iguana's cage.
Nice try, though.

                    Love,
                    Mom

Dear Alex,

Tarantulas are quiet too, but I wouldn't want one as a pet. By the way, that iguana of Mikey's is uglier than Godzilla. Just thought I'd mention it.

Love,
Mom

Dear Mom,

You would never even have to see the iguana. I'll keep his cage in my room on the dresser next to my soccer trophies. Plus, he's so small, I bet you'll never even know he's there.

Love and a zillion and one kisses,

Alex

Dear Alex,

Iguanas can grow to be over six feet long. You won't have enough space in your whole room, much less on your dresser (with or without your trophies).

Love,
Mom

Dear Mom,

It takes 15 years for an iguana to get that big. Mikey told me. I'll be married by then and probably living in my own house.

Love,
Your smart and mature kid, Alex

Dear Alex,

How are you going to get

a girl to marry you when

you own a six-foot-long

reptile?

Love,

Your concerned mother

Dear Mom,
Forget the girl.
I need a new friend now!

This iguana can be the brother I've always wanted.

Love,

Your lonely child, Alex

Dear Mom,
I know I have a brother
but he's just a baby.
What fun is that? If I had
an iguana, I could teach
it tricks and things.
Ethan doesn't do tricks.
He just burps and poops.

Love,
Grossed-out Alex

Dear Alex,
How do I know you're ready for a pet? Remember what happened when you took home the class fish?
Love,
Mom

Dear Mom,

If I knew the fish was going to jump into the spaghetti sauce, I never would have taken the cover off the jar!

Love,
Your son who has learned his lesson

P.S. Iguanas don't like spaghetti.

Dear Alex,
Let's say I let you have
the iguana on a trial basis.
What exactly would you do
to take care of it?
Love,
Mom

Dear Mom,
I would feed him every day (he eats lettuce). And I would make sure he had enough water. And I would clean his cage when it got messy.

Love,
Responsible Alex
P.S. What's a trial basis?

Dear Alex,

A trial basis means Dad and I see how well you take care of him for a week or two before we decide if you can have him forever. Remember, Stinky and Lurch are waiting!

Love,
Mom

P.S. If you clean his cage as well as you clean your room, you're in trouble.

Dear Mom,

I'll really, really, really try to clean my room and the iguana's cage. Also, I'll pay for the lettuce with my allowance. I mean, how much can one baby iguana eat, anyway?

Love,
Alex the financial wizard

"Are you sure you want to do this, Alex?"

"Yes, Mom!
I wanna iguana. . . . .
Please!"

Dear Alex,

Look on your dresser.

Love,
Mom

"YESSSS!
Thank you!
Thank
you!"